**William Procter**

# The Hygiene of Air and Water

Anatiposi

William Procter

# The Hygiene of Air and Water

Reprint of the original, first published in 1872.

1st Edition 2023 | ISBN: 978-3-38213-010-7

Anatiposi Verlag is an imprint of Outlook Verlagsgesellschaft mbH.

Verlag (Publisher): Outlook Verlag GmbH, Zeilweg 44, 60439 Frankfurt, Deutschland
Vertretungsberechtigt (Authorized to represent): E. Roepke, Zeilweg 44, 60439 Frankfurt, Deutschland
Druck (Print): Books on Demand GmbH, In de Tarpen 42, 22848 Norderstedt, Deutschland

THE

# HYGIENE OF AIR AND WATER:

BEING A POPULAR ACCOUNT OF THE

## EFFECTS OF THE IMPURITIES OF AIR AND WATER,

## THEIR DETECTION,

## AND THE MODES OF REMEDYING THEM.

BY

# WILLIAM PROCTER, M.D., F.C.S.,

SURGEON TO THE YORK DISPENSARY,

AND FORMERLY LECTURER ON CHEMISTRY AND FORENSIC MEDICINE

IN THE YORK SCHOOL OF MEDICINE.

LONDON:

R. HARDWICKE.

YORK:

J. SAMPSON, E. PICKERING, JOHNSON & TESSEYMAN.

1872.

TO

GEORGE SHANN, Esq., M.D.,

THIS SMALL VOLUME IS DEDICATED,

IN GRATEFUL ACKNOWLEDGMENT OF MANY ACTS OF

PERSONAL AND PROFESSIONAL KINDNESS

RENDERED TO HIS OBLIGED FRIEND

THE AUTHOR.

# PREFACE.

The matter of this small volume was contained in a series of letters which were published by the Author in the York newspapers. It was thought, by some clerical and other friends, that the information contained in them should assume a more permanent place in a manual for general use and parochial distribution. At their request the treatment of the subject has been enlarged for production in the present form. As treated in the following pages, the subject admits of no originality, and the Author claims none; his object has been to deal with it in as simple and popular a manner as possible, and to point out the injurious effects produced on health by impure air and water, the sources and origin of their impurities, with the means for their detection, and the several methods by which they may be removed or remedied.

# THE IMPURITIES OF AIR,

### AND

# THEIR REMOVAL.

**Causes of Atmospheric Impurity.**—The atmosphere constituting the air which we breathe is a mixture of several gases, two of which are constant in quantity, the others being variable. The two constant constituents are Oxygen and Nitrogen, in the proportions of 21 of the former to 79 of the latter. On Oxygen depend the active properties of air. It is necessary to the breathing of man and animals, its exclusion rapidly produces death, and it is the essential cause of many changes effected by the atmosphere. The variable constituents are watery vapour and carbonic acid gas. The quantity of the former varies from $\frac{1}{3}$ to 2 per cent., and is regulated mainly by temperature. Carbonic acid is a heavy, highly poisonous gas, varying from 2 to 5 volumes in 10,000 volumes of air. Air, which contains 50 to 100 per 10,000 volumes, is fatal to life; but in considerably less quantity it is adverse to comfort and obnoxious to health. In addition to these ingredients, Ammonia, and a very energetic form of Oxygen, called Ozone, are present in small quantities. This latter substance is evolved when the electrical machine is in action, and is most readily prepared by placing a clean stick of Phosphorus, almost covered by distilled water, in a large bottle of air, with a close-fitting stopper. When the bottle is kept at about 65° for thirty or forty minutes, the air becomes ozonized. It has energetic chemical powers, but the property of most interest here is that of destroying all foul organic effluvia. It is the great scavenging agent of Nature, and is generated, probably, by atmospheric electrical disturbances. To discover the presence of Ozone in the air, strips of paper, or calico, should be soaked in the following mixture :—Dissolve 10 grains of *pure* Iodide of Potassium in 2,000 grains of distilled water ; add 100 grains of starch, and heat gently. On exposure to the air, if Ozone is present, the slip will be browned, the intensity of colour being dependent upon the quantity existing. Ozone abounds in sea air, but is not found in the air of towns, and its presence or absence is intimately associated with the occurrence of certain epidemic diseases. Besides these essential components of air, portions of all substances capable of being suspended or dissolved as vapours in this aeriform mixture may also be present, and a brief consideration will show that the causes are very numerous which tend to produce vitiation by the introduction of accidental constituents. The result is, that in proportion to the degree of contamination, pure air, essential for our well-being, loses the balance of composition demanded for perfect health, and becomes, more or less, pernicious. Whatever may be the nature or origin of this deleterious matter, it is introduced, by breathing, into the blood whilst passing through the lungs, which present an absorbing surface of at least from 10 to 20 square feet.

We now proceed to consider more in detail the principal causes which operate in rendering air impure. One great cause is found in ourselves.

**Effects of Respiration.**—Breathing, or respiration, consists of two acts :—(1) Inspiration, taking pure air into the lungs by the expansion of the chest; and (2), Expelling it from the lungs in an impure state, called Expiration. This impure state is chiefly caused by the highly poisonous gas, Carbonic Acid, with which the expired air has become charged, and which will be, presently, more fully considered. But this is not the only mischief; for, in addition to the air being deprived of its vital Oxygen, which is replaced by Carbonic Acid, a variable quantity of animal (organic) matter accompanies it from the lungs ; the latter, on an average, may be estimated at thirty or forty grains a day for each adult. It consists of small particles of skin (epithelium), fatty matters, and a peculiar fetid (organic) vapour, the cause of the disagreeable odour in close and crowded rooms, which gives rise, by its decomposition, to products detrimental to health. If this air is passed through water, the latter soon exhibits all the phenomena of putrefactive fermentation. The water given out also in respiration is thus loaded with animal impurities, condenses on the inner walls of buildings, and trickles down in fetid streams. In the close and confined dwellings of the poor, the vapour collects on the walls, ceiling, and furniture, making them clammy to the touch, and giving that permanent loathsome odour which must be familiar to those who are acquainted with such localities.

removal of these obstacles to health, the rural plague has disappeared, and the visitation not been repeated.

**Sewer Gas and its Remedies.**—Sewers, it is evident, form large reservoirs for the emanations under consideration; and in towns, from various reasons, there is always a liability to the escape of sewer air into houses. Under these influences the general health is affected, but there is connected with it a matter of greater consequence in relation to the close intimacy which exists between typhoid fever and sewage exhalation. Whether this matter is simply the means of conveying the specific poison derived from the evacuations passed into the sewers, or whether such matter is capable itself of setting up fever, is an unsettled question; and, therefore, in a state of doubt, it is necessary to look upon these emanations with the greatest suspicion, for they certainly can give rise to diarrhœa, bilious disorders, &c., and promote the diffusion and extension of all diseases. Dr. H. Barker showed the effects of sewer air, by conducting the gases from a cesspool into a closed box, in which animals were confined; some were killed, whilst others —three dogs—suffered from vomiting and purging, and a febrile condition similar to the milder forms of continued fever common to the dirty and ill-ventilated houses of the lower class of the community. Dr. Letheby says that ordinary London sewage disengages from 1 to 1¼ cubic feet* of gas per hour per gallon, composed of light Carburetted Hydrogen, Car-

---

* Cubic inches and cubic feet are represented by " C.I." and " C.F." in subsequent pages. .

bonic Acid, Sulphuretted Hydrogen alone and with Ammonia. These gases are all more or less poisonous, and with them is mingled a putrid organic vapour. But the exact composition of the gaseous contents of a sewer will depend upon ventilation; or, in other words, the extent to which the vapours are withdrawn and their place supplied by pure air. The importance of this, in a sanatory point of view, cannot be over estimated. Mr. Latham writes thus :—"Having examined hundreds of houses in which typhoid fever has occurred, I have always been able to trace the outbreak either to some unlooked-for defect in house drainage, or the public system of sewage with which the drains were connected. In ninety-nine cases out of a hundred, I have found them free from deposit, and the traps in all cases perfect ; but a more careful examination soon showed that the absence of ventilation was the sole cause of the disease." The gases generated by decomposition rise to the upper part of the drain or sewer, and there is great danger of them passing into the house, even if traps are used to close the openings, as all traps are frequently unable to resist the gas pressure to which they may be submitted, a danger greatly increased by the existence of any impediment to gas escape at the sewer outlet. Again, the water constituting the traps absorbs the gases ; when this is saturated, it may become a centre of mischief by yielding emanations. No trap can prevent at least the occasional entrance of sewer gas into a house. A flap-trap is not closed at all times, and is never stronger than the weight of a column of water 1½ inch high, while bell-traps are rarely stronger than a column one quarter of an inch high, and yet Mr. Latham tells us that the expansive force of gases in a sewer sometimes exceeds the weight of a column of water 30 inches high. Therefore, to relieve any possible pressure on the traps, other means of exit should be provided by the use of ventilating shafts. This can be carried out in many ways ; such, for instance, as by a pipe passing from the sewer into the air above the houses ; and it has been proposed to increase the draught by conducting the openings into chimneys or furnaces. In the former case, there will be danger of down draught in the absence of fires, and in the latter case, if the openings are numerous, the action is inefficient. In practice there is a difficulty in forcing the air of a large system of sewers into ventilating shafts ; and even when this is managed, the mischief is not avoided, as an accumulation takes place in branch drains. Dr. Carpenter, of Croydon, where the plan has been successfully carried out, proposes to remedy the evils arising from the escape of noxious gases through traps, by discharging them just before they reach that part of the house. His plan consists in making an opening into the pipes below the traps, or soil pipe of the water-closet, and carrying another pipe from thence to the roof. The gases then at once escape by the open pipe into the upper air. The effect of this arrangement, the proposer says, is that there are no longer any closed portions of pipe in which air can remain stagnant, and the conditions required for the generation of foul gas no longer exist. A complete circulation of air is established throughout the whole system of drains, large and small. The openings in our streets through which noxious fumes now arise, become inlets for pure air, which will force its way through these household ventilating shafts. " If this principle is carried out in a district containing 8,000 houses, if each house averages five communications with the house drains, it follows that 40,000 openings will exist, which should rise above the level of the highest windows, but not on a level with the tops of the chimneys. These 40,000 openings will ensure a positive circulation in all the house drains by reason of natural laws, which are always in operation, such as the tendency of air at different temperatures, and at different degrees of saturation, as regards moisture to commingle ; of gases of different densities to diffuse themselves, which action will be constantly assisted by the motion of the external air. These forces will, together, compel a circulation, and prevent the possibility of that stagnation which allows of fungoid growth, upon which the development of sewer gas sometimes depends, and the concentration of the latter in a manner dangerous to those who come in contact with it." Recent circumstances have caused much attention to be drawn to house drains and their connection with sewers, and have called forth, in the public prints, opinions and practical advice from many of our most eminent engineers. The great teaching to be drawn is :—(1) That no sewers, or drains, or pipes, should run into drains in dwelling houses. (2) If this is impracticable, all sink pipes or waste pipes should be broken off at least one foot above the trapped grating into which they discharge. (3) On no account should a cesspool be placed within the walls of a dwelling, but as far as possible from the house. It is a mistake to cover them up closely; let them, writes Mr. Rawlinson, be abundantly ventilated to the external air. Whatever drains run into them should be so ventilated, or broken at the upper surface, that they do not form a continuous flue through which the cesspool gas can possibly pass to and within the house. All sewers should daily have a large quantity of water passing through them, and if there should be suspicion of disease caused by the gases, in the examination particular attention should be paid to the general construction of the sewers, and their fall, their terminations, their trapping, their ventilation, and the amount of water passing through them. As an adjunct to the ventilation of sewers, the employment of charcoal is of the highest value. In 1854, Dr. Stenhouse showed that if putrid air was slowly passed through charcoal, the poisonous and offensive gases were entirely destroyed, and he was, hence, led to devise the charcoal air filter. This consists essentially of a layer of charcoal interposed between two sheets of wire gauze, supported in a suitable frame of metal or wood. Mr. Haywood and Dr. Letheby have reported on the use of these filters in London: they employed wood charcoal, broken into pieces the size of a filbert. It was packed closely, but without compression, upon the various trays, and each tray held about 1¹⁄₁₆ lb. of charcoal, making altogether 6½lbs. distributed over the six trays of each air filter. These closely fitted on the ventilated opening of a sewer, take all pressure off the water traps, and preserve their power for years. The conclusions of the reporters are, " that the charcoal filters may be used with efficacy in the course of the air channels from the drains and closets of houses, as well as in the ventilation of public sewers ; that in applying the charcoal, those contrivances should be used which offer the least resistance to the free passage of the air; that the situation of the filters is best where the charcoal is protected from wet and from dirt, and is easily accessible ; that from the ascertained efficacy of the charcoal, in destroying the dangerous emanations from sewers, the system may be generally applied with great advantage." Mr. Rawlinson employs them in the sewers of every town which he drains.

General Considerations.—The liability to the causes of impurity we have been considering, is much less probable in the free atmosphere of rural districts than in the confined localities of towns. But under either condition, great care and attention are requisite to prevent their influence in the abodes of sickness and disease, for in them exist additional morbid exhalations from the body of the patient, and effluvia from discharged excretions ; such, and other, circumstances largely increasing the probability of bad effects. Mr. Condy has suggested a general method for the detection of an impure condition of the atmosphere, based upon the fact that his red fluid (solution of permanganate of potash) is decolorized in contact with organic matter. Place, he says, in a line four or more perfectly clean dishes of white ware. Into each pour an ounce of distilled water. To the first then add a drop of Condy's fluid, diluted previously with two

B

parts of water; to the second add two drops, and so on
according to the number of vessels. Let the dishes so
prepared stand for a time in a quiet part of the room.
On examining them at the end of the period, the state of
the atmosphere, during exposure, can be judged of. If
the solution in No. 1 has not entirely lost its pink colour,
the purity of the air is normal; should No. 2 be decolorized, the air must have been loaded with twice as great an
amount of impurity, and so the loss of colour in the
others will demonstrate degrees of impurity verging more
or less on to positive pollution. This plan is not admis-
sible for scientific purposes, but sufficiently accurate for
ordinary sanitary objects. "By practice, this'method is
capable, in the hands of any person of common intelli-
gence, of rendering important service in the management
of the sick room, and, by its means, the occurrence of
even a temporary undue accumulation of foul air can be
rendered apparent."

The general facts deducible from the preceding considerations are, that whatever may be the extraordinary
causes of epidemics of an atmospheric kind, the sources
of a very large proportion of ordinary disorders are
found in the putrifying filth of one kind and another,
which the negligence of our poorer fellow-countrymen
allows to accumulate around, about, and sometimes
in, their dwellings. But this charge cannot be made
against them alone, for too often those who have
the direction of sanitary matters in our towns and cities
are open to similar blame, by their neglect of the most
obvious means for the preservation of the health of the

inhabitants. In a general sense, it is certain that filth and disease stand in the relation of cause and effect, and that poverty, although often the first, is not the only victim; so that the negligence of the upper and lower classes of society alike, in these matters, entails terrible calamities on both. The fevers and contagious disorders arising from the neglect of the poor, either on their own or on our part, find their way into the dwellings of all classes, and equally establish disease. The poorer class cannot with impunity live in a state of unnecessary filth and dirt; neither, on the other hand, may the rich without danger neglect the sanitary and physical conditions of the poor around them. Both are subject to the same natural laws, which must be obeyed; and neglect of these laws bears its own punishment. Such principles fully carried out afford the most certain security against the invasion of formidable disease.

**Natural Laws for the Purification of the Atmosphere.**—Certain physical laws are established by which injurious atmospheric agents can be destroyed or overcome; and did these not exist, the whole human race would eventually succumb to their deleterious influence.

These laws are of two kinds.

(1) The production of atmospheric currents, or winds, by the influence of which the impure air is being continually replaced by that which is pure, carrying away the agents of mischief, or diluting them to such a degree that they are rendered innocuous. These may be called the mechanical agents of purification, but they have also a chemical aspect.

Whilst Oxygen, as already mentioned, either alone or under the form of Ozone, is an essential constituent of the atmosphere, it is at the same time the great purifier. Through its agency all occasional ingredients of the air, noxious or otherwise, can, by a process called oxidation, be reduced to simpler and simpler forms, until, eventually, they are rendered inert. The atmosphere is, then, not only a grand receptacle, but also the laboratory for the decomposition, of substances finding their way into it, converting noxious into harmless compounds, which are not useless, but, being washed down by the freshening rain, supply a fertilizing fluid to the roots of vegetables, minister to their growth, and finally furnish, through the medium of the plant, food to man and other animals. Properly managed, these emanations of death and decay are a part of the vast plan by which the balance of organic nature is maintained, and it is our duty to aid the attainment of this end by their proper distribution through the atmosphere.

(2) The second law to which allusion has been made is that which is called Diffusion, meaning in reality a property which gases and vapours have of spreading or diffusing themelves through each other. By virtue of this force the heaviest gases rise in the air, and the most dense and the most rare gradually mix with each other, the effect being the dispersion of vaporous matter and the dilution of the injurious air by that which is pure and wholesome.

Ventilation.—Such are the self-acting modes of purification with which nature has furnished the atmosphere for the preservation of man's health. But in houses the same purifying conditions do not exist, and the confined space renders contamination and its bad effects more probable. If, then, free circulation of air in our streets removes impurities, and is otherwise conducive to health, it is called for more imperatively in our dwellings, and, in consequence, we imitate these natural agencies by artificial ventilation.

Fully to appreciate the importance of ventilation, it is necessary to consider in detail a few of the sources of contamination to which our habitations are subjected. On an average, a man breathes 28,800 C.I., or 16·66 C.F. of air per hour, and produces in twenty-four hours 12 to 16 C.F. of Carbonic Acid gas. To dilute this quantity to a safe limit, so that the Carbonic Acid does not exceed 0·4 per thousand of air, there should be supplied at least 100 times the volume of the air expired, or more than 1,666 C.F. of air per hour ; but as other sources of vitiation are present, such as artificial combustion, exhalation of the skin, &c., the amount should really be 2,802 C.F. per hour (Parkes). In sickness, the causes of vitiation being clearly more abundant, a larger supply is needed. Dr. Sutherland says, that, under such circumstances, not less than 4,500 C.F. should be furnished in the same time, and during epidemics at least 6,000 C.F. Closely allied to contamination of air by respiration is that produced by combustion. A cubic foot of coal gas will, on an average, give, when burnt, 2 C.F. of Carbonic Acid with about ½ grain of Sulphurous Acid, and this will require at the least 1,800 C.F. of air to dilute it to a healthy standard. An ordinary sitting-room burner consumes 3 C.F. of gas per hour. Very similar products (except the sulphur compound) are formed by the burning of oil, candles, &c.

The amount of air furnished to each person in a given apartment is found by multiplying the dimensions of length, breadth, and height, and dividing the product by the number of persons. By law these dimensions regulate the quantity of air to be supplied to each person in lodging-houses, barracks, &c. The Poor Law Board allows 300 C.F. for every healthy person in dormitories, and 500 C.F. for every sick person; whilst in permanent barracks, each man is allowed 600 C.F. But the quantity alone is not all important; the removal of the air is quite as essential, for the purpose of removing or diluting to the degree already stated the products of respiration, perspiration, combustion,. &c.

This renewal of air is effected by ventilation, which is of two kinds:

(1.) Natural ventilation, effected by windows, doors, and crevices, as inlets; and chimneys and fireplaces, as outlets,

(2) Artificial ventilation, which is usually effected by the action of valves, fans, &c., stoves, or other artificial heat, including gas, whereby air is either drawn into, or forced out of, an apartment. The fundamental principles of ventilation, simple as they are, should never be forgotten, and may be stated in a few words. Whenever air is heated, it expands, and,. becoming lighter, ascends, producing a space more or less empty. To supply the vacuum thus caused, the surrounding cold air

rushes in. This process going on in the atmosphere around us, constitutes a wind or current of air. This natural law is imitated in our dwellings, for the purpose of purifying the air which we have contaminated ; thus, when a fire is lighted in a grate, the air in the chimney becomes heated and ascends, its place being supplied by the external air rushing in through the crevices of the window and door, and flowing up the chimney. The process continues as long as the fire is burning in the grate, and as long as the foul air drawn into the chimney is heated and expanded on its arrival there. The desired exchange is now produced, and will continue, provided the conditions on which it depends, viz., a supply of colder air, meets with no interference. But it will not go on when the air to be changed is equal in temperature to, or colder than the external air ; therefore the change is most active in winter, when rooms are artificially warmed ; and least so in hot weather, when the external and internal temperatures approximate each other, or are similar. It is probable that, in most dwelling rooms, provided as they are with tolerably large open fire-places, and with doors which are frequently opened, the ventilation is, under ordinary circumstances, sufficiently complete; while it is in crowded rooms that assistance is more especially demanded. In considering the subject in detail, the first point is the introduction of the air. When it enters at the windows and doors in the manner previously mentioned, and when no other arrangement exists, draughts are certain to be established, more or less, according to the size. &c., of the apertures. It may seem singular that a room insufficiently supplied with air may be draughty, but, nevertheless, it is a fact. If, when a fire is burning in a room, as much air cannot enter as passes away by the chimney, the pressure of air within is diminished, and the outer air then rushes in with violence through every available crevice or aperture, and draughts are established. The question how and where to introduce the cold air, required for ventilation and combustion, in an imperceptible manner, is difficult to solve, and is not settled in a satisfactory manner. The main points demanding attention are the equal distribution of the current, by causing the air to pass through a large number of apertures, such as wire gauze, perforated zinc, and the like, and the employment of adequate means to bring it to a suitable temperature, by being made to circulate through boxes heated by steam pipes, &c., or through chambers behind or around stoves, grates, &c. If the air cannot be heated, it should then be brought into the room 9 or 10 feet from the floor, a direction towards the ceiling being given to it, so that it may pass upwards, then fall, and gradually mix with the air of the room. Windows properly constructed, made to open *above* and *below*, and suitably placed, afford the most ready means for the natural ventilation of dwellings. The air is better directed and distributed by making the top sash of the window open slopingly by a lever and pivot, the pivot being placed, not in the centre, but at the bottom of the sash, by which the down draught is avoided ; or a board may be placed obliquely from the top sash of the window, when it is open in the usual manner. By either of these contrivances, the incoming current is directed to the ceiling, is divided, and has its velocity checked. To fulfil the same object, a number of holes are bored obliquely through the panes, or glass louvres, variously fashioned, which can be more or less closed, are placed in the windows. Lockhead's (fig. 1) ventilator is a pane of perforated glass, in a metal frame, with a hinged cover, which can be raised, so that the air can be admitted as desired. Another mode of regulating the entrance of air, is by means of a plate of glass, made to turn, so that the openings in the glass may be partially or entirely opened or closed. Wire gauze admits of many applications, and may be placed before louvres or other openings, to distribute more equally the entering air.* Louvre boards may be placed above a doorway, and, though not very sightly, are very efficient. Mr. Cooke recommends air to be admitted through wire gauze (fig. 2), arranged in a window in folds, and fitted with joints in such a manner, that when the sash is opened, the gauze becomes more or less expanded, and when closed, the gauze becomes doubled up on itself. Boyle's ventilator (fig. 6) consists of an ornamental disc of glass, covering an opening in the window of wire gauze; the former admits of being pulled forward, by which the quantity of air admitted can be regulated. Fig 7 consists of perforated metal in a window by which air passes in, the quantity being regulated by a slide covering the apertures. But a little ingenuity will enable any person, by the aid of perforated zinc or glass, or wire gauze and sliding valves,

---

* Figures of many of these applications will be found in the excellent work on Ventilation, by Mr. Edwards.

to make any arrangement he requires, when he understands the principles of ventilator construction. Rooms in which a fire is burning can be readily furnished with a supply of warm air for ventilation, by conveying it through a pipe, or chamber, formed under the floor, or in the wall, leading to an air chamber at the back or sides of the stove, in order that it may be warmed before entering the room (fig 3), and, by a little contrivance, warm air may be made to feed the fire. An independent supply of this kind is calculated to prevent the chimney from smoking, and to secure economy of fuel, as well as freedom from cold draughts passing from the windows and doors to the fire.

Numerous inventions have been patented for the introduction of air into apartments without draught. In this place it is, for want of space, impossible to do more than notice briefly two or three of the simpler methods. The one approved by the Barrack Commissioners is this :—At the level of the ceiling, perforated bricks are introduced into the wall, the area of aperture being usually 1 sq. inch to every 60 C.F. of the capacity of the room (fig 4). To prevent the down draught, a cornice is arranged to cover the openings, having its upper side made of perforated zinc.

A simple plan, which works well in schools, has been proposed by Mr. H. Varley. A perforated zinc tube, opening into the external air, passes round the cornice of three sides of the room ; on the fourth side, another perforated tube is connected with the chimney. Fig 5 is an arrangement by which air can be admitted independently of the window-sash. Air from without passes into a small chamber, and through gauze, which can be adapted to regulate the quantity of air entering the room.

The examples which have been given will serve to illustrate the principles of the plans to be adopted for the ingress of the air required for ventilation; and we have now to direct attention to the egress of the lighter and contaminated air. In arranging the inlets and outlets, certain conditions should be borne in mind, viz., to have the incoming air pure; to aid distribution, the inlets should be numerous and small, and turn upwards to lessen the probability of draughts; and it may be advisable to have the external openings provided with means of closing them in very cold or windy weather. The incoming air is to be distributed equally, and the position and sizes of the inlets and outlets should be so arranged that the currents are kept vertical. It is important to be careful that the supply is in sufficient quantity to drive out and replace the vitiated air, otherwise the latter will collect at the top of the room, and eventually be diffused through its entire space. Neglect of this consideration is one of the reasons why ventilation is inefficiently carried out in practice; the inlet should be at least 1 sq. inch for every 60 C.F. capacity. Reed says that 10 C.F. should be supplied to each individual per minute. Dr. Parkes says that the size of the apertures will have to depend upon the temperature and height of the column. If the height of a heated column be 15 ft., and a difference exists of ten degrees between external and internal temperature, and if the discharge per man be 2,000 C.F. per hour, the outlet space per man will require to be 24 square inches, nearly equivalent to an opening 5 inches square. There must be of course an equal amount of inlet, so that the inlet and outlet together would be 48 square inches per head. This, therefore, would be the total open area necessary for each person, independently of all openings by windows and doors. To get the total size of the openings for any room containing healthy persons, multiply 48 by the number of persons, and the result will be the total section area to be provided, expressed in square inches. For hospitals, multiply 72 by the number of persons. The same author goes on to say that it is commonly stated, that as the heated air expands, the outlets should be larger than the inlets, and the great disproportions, 5 to 4 and 10 to 9, have been given. In practice, he thinks this may be disregarded, and that the inlets and outlets may be of the same size. It is desirable to make each inlet opening not larger than from 48 to 60 square inches, and the outlet not more than 1 square foot. The outlet is more certain and constant in its action, if the air can be warmed—a fact exemplified in the chimney and open fire, which carries on the removal most efficiently. Gas for this purpose admits of extensive application. A good and simple arrangement is to place over the gas jet a pipe, to carry off the products of combustion, and to case this pipe in a tube which opens on the ceiling. Two outlet currents are thus established, one over the gas, and one through the outer tube. Rickett's ventilating globe light (in reality the invention of Faraday) is on this principle, its only objection being its expense. A somewhat similar contrivance, the " sunlight" method of illumination, is one of the best modes of ventilation. It consists in the gas being burnt under an opening in the ceiling, the opening being furnished with a pipe for conveying away the products of combustion, &c. In all these, and like arrangements, care should be taken that the channel for the escape of air from the room is of sufficient size, and that it inclines at an angle towards the chimney, otherwise the water of combustion, condensing within it, may form an obstruction.

Numerous ventilating valves, or combinations of tubes, &c., of various kinds, have been proposed to aid the removal of tainted air. It is impossible, in the present limited space, to give a detailed account of these contrivances. The one best known, and, at the same time, simple and inexpensive, is that suggested by Dr. Arnott. It consists in making an opening into the chimney, near the ceiling, and fixing a balancing valve in it in such a manner that the valve plate is opened by outward draughts, but closed by those from within. For the same purpose, the plan is modified by use of perforated zinc as a ventilator, and the action of Arnott's valve is imitated, by a valve of oiled silk, or valves of mica. For the proper working of these ventilators, the throat of the chimney, just over the fire, should be contracted, and then a low arch should be fixed, as a sort of blower, over the top bar of the grate, to quicken and steady the draught. It is worse than useless to put one into a chimney where the fireplace is large and open. As long as a body of air, filling the whole chimney, passes freely through it from the fireplace, none will pass through the ventilator, and smoke may find its way through the latter into the room; but if the fireplace is contracted, part of the air will go over the fire, and part will flow steadily through the valve.

When the external air is warm and free from motion, it becomes more difficult to secure the free ventilation of rooms. Under these circumstances, as in summer, the only natural mode of ventilation is through open windows, and there can be no better method, unless this is supplemented by some artificial contrivance. Unnecessary fear prevails generally in relation to open windows; of the two, it is certainly better to breathe air moistened with night-dew than that laden with poison vapours. At night the central air shaft of gaslights may be made available. The chimney is thought to produce a current outwards, but it is often the reverse. A draught as often comes *into* as passes *out* of the room through this aperture, a defect admitting of remedy by keeping a small gas or other lamp burning in the grate; an out-draught is thus established without increasing the temperature of the room, and at a very small expense the gas can be supplied by a flexible tube, passing from a neighbouring supply pipe. A contrivance of the Marquis de Chabannes is very useful. About the height of the mantel-piece (fig 9), an opening was made into the chimney. At the mouth of it was placed a lamp, partly enclosed in a case of metal, and so arranged that whilst it lighted the apartment, it at the same time effected ventilation, by setting up a current of heated air, which passed into the chimney. These modes of ventilation in bedrooms, and in those of sick persons, are excellent.

The preceding considerations teach that the atmospheric purifying agencies of Nature are diffusion, dilution, oxidation, and washing by rain; and those who value health, and wish, as far as possible, to breathe untainted air, should introduce into their dwellings as liberal a supply of fresh air as can be obtained without discomfort.

Disinfectants.—But in the apartments of the sick, other considerations demand attention. It is a certain fact, that the presence of organic matters, floating in the air, are the great means by which many diseases are disseminated. Of this character are the specific poisons of certain fevers, measles, small-pox, and the like,—and some of these even appear to defy the effects of ventilation, whilst others readily yield to its influence. As examples of the former may be mentioned small-pox and scarlet fever; for, in spite of ventilation, the air long retains a power of setting up these diseases. Fortunately, we are in possession of a class of agents which are capable of destroying, more or less completely, infectious matter of this character. Such are disinfectants; and closely allied to them is another class—deodorisers, which have the property of removing offensive smells without of necessity affecting the active agents of disease. In the broadest sense, then, a disinfectant is anything which counteracts infectious, contagious, or effete matters. Disinfectants may be said to act on infectious matter in one of two ways. (1) By a process of oxidation, which effects the decay or decomposition of organic matter, resolving it into harmless products. These are **Disinfect-ants proper.** (2) By preventing putrefaction and fermentation or any change from taking place in the original composition of the organic matter. These are **Antiseptics, or Colytics.** To these divisions another may practically be added, to which the term **Fixative** has been applied; one or more of the constituents of these agents combines with the offensive volatile pro-ducts, *fixes* them, and prevents the pollution of the air by their escape : such are Burnett's Fluid, many metallic salts, &c.

It is only possible to consider the subject briefly, with respect to the use of ordinary disinfectants, and the cir-cumstances under which their employment is specially indicated.

**Chlorine** is an energetic destroyer of all organic substances prone to decay, and acts on offensive gases, the result of putrefaction. It is one of the most valuable atmospheric disinfectants and deodorisers, but demands, at least in its pure state, to be used cautiously, on account of the unpleasant effects produced by it on the organs of respiration. For use, it may be thus prepared :—Place equal parts of common salt and black oxide of man-ganese in a basin, pour in some water, and then add an equal quantity, or less, of oil of vitriol, and the gas is given off. The rapidity of the evolution of gas may be diminished by the addition of water. There are many cases in which the so-called **Chloride of Lime** may, with advantage, be substituted, especially when a solution is required, in the proportion of one pound to a gallon of water. Its unpleasant sickly odour can be overcome by the addition of a small quantity of Nitro-Benzole. For general purposes, if there is sufficient Chlorine to give an odour of the gas, it is in sufficient quantity to disinfect. Chlorine, but not pure, may be evolved by the addition of an acid to Chloride of Lime. Mr. Condy has suggested an elegant means of Chloridizing. Into a cup, placed on a plate, a wineglass-full of Condy's fluid is poured; on the addition, gradually, of a small portion of Muriatic Acid, the gas is given off until the ingredients are exhausted.

On account of the irrespirable nature of Chlorine, a good substitute for it is found in **Iodine.** Some of this substance is placed in saucers, in different parts of the room, it evaporates spontaneously, and the characteristic odour is soon perceptible, or the diffusion may be accelerated by the application of slight heat.

Alkaline manganates and permanganates have been introduced by Mr. Condy, under the title of **Condy's Fluid,** red and green. As disinfectants, they are invaluable and elegant, admitting of a wide range of application. It is needless here to describe either their uses or mode of application, as full directions are given with the preparations, which are essential to every household.

**The Antiseptics, or Colytics,** are a class which have the power of preventing organic substances from undergoing change. Disinfectants proper exercise their influence upon substances, or products, which are the results of changes already effected; whilst antiseptics

c

*prevent* these results, by arresting decay and decomposition. So that whilst an antiseptic preserves from putrefaction, it does not of necessity remove the odour of that matter which has previously undergone change.

**Heat and Cold** are natural antiseptics. Extreme cold prevents animal poisons from being diffused and oxidised, and therefore restrains putrefaction. The greater number of animal substances may be indefinitely preserved at or below the freezing point; but with an elevation of temperature, the liability to undergo change or decomposition returns. Extreme heat destroys the structure of poisons, and may, in a general manner, operate beneficially by producing expansion, and consequent dilution, of the noxious material. It is to the late Dr. Henry that we are indebted for a knowledge of the powerful destructive influence exerted by dry heat upon the specific poisons of disease. Vaccine virus was deprived of the power of reproduction after exposure to a temperature of 140° for three hours ; but this result did not follow when the heat did not exceed 120°. From this and similar facts, he was led to suggest the adoption of a method for the disinfection of clothing, and the like, which consists in exposing them to a temperature of 212° to 214° in a chamber built of brick, the floor of which is composed of perforated iron plate. Below this is a coil of iron pipe, which acts as part of a furnace flue, radiating heat into the compartment. Experience has fully corroborated the success of this plan, when carried out with proper care, and for a sufficiently long time. In the absence of a chamber, an oven, cautiously heated, may be employed, the articles being kept in the heated air for at least two hours.

It is greatly to be regretted that every town in the kingdom is not furnished with some such apparatus, for there is little doubt that its general use would do much to diminish the spread of infectious disease.

**The Fumes of Burning Sulphur** (Sulphurous Acid) have very powerful disinfecting properties; they are effectual, economical, of considerable permanence, and can be readily applied. The same may be said of **Nitrous fumes.** The chief objections are the poisonous and irrespirable properties of the gases, which render their employment impracticable, except in uninhabited places. **Carbolic Acid,** even when highly diluted, is most destructive to all the lower forms of animal and vegetable life, and arrests and prevents all kinds of putrefactive changes; its vapour has the same action, and it is in every respect a true antiseptic. The Disinfectant Powders of Calvert and Mc.Dougall (the former being more efficacious, with a less unpleasant odour) are compounds of the Sulphites and Carbolic Acid, and act most advantageously when a powder is demanded for the disinfection of masses of putrescent matter, stables, sewage, or fecal matter. They influence also the surrounding atmosphere, and have still further the valuable property of absorbing moisture, thus removing a condition most favourable for putrefactive action.

The use of **Fixatives,** such as the **Sulphates of Iron and Zinc, Chloride of Iron, Burnett's Fluid,** &c., is indicated when large masses of putrefying matter have to be disinfected for a time, and at a small cost. The Chloride of Aluminium, or **Chloralum**, is one of this class lately introduced. It possesses several advantages ; it is not poisonous, is inodorous, and is very cheap. The great use of it is for the prevention of decomposition, and to remove the fœtor of most animal discharges, either natural or the products of disease. It deodorises sewage, and may be used for the disinfection of rooms, when mixed with water, and used as a cleansing material. Not being volatile, it is probably inferior to some other agents as an aerial disinfectant.

In practically carrying out disinfection, it is to be remembered that the process is not a simple one, but depends upon varying and complex chemical and physiological actions, and that varying products and different circumstances will have to be dealt with. The attempt, therefore, to obtain a disinfectant of universal application, and capable of fulfilling every indication, must be attended with disappointment. The relative value of the substances which have been mentioned, in preventing putrefaction, may be taken as a test of their action on the germs of infection. Dr. Crace Calvert has published experiments, in which meat was suspended in bottles over the various substances with the following results :—

| Antiseptic used. | Became tainted. | Putrid. |
|---|---|---|
| Condy's Fluid ........ | 2 days ........ | 4 days |
| Chloralum .......... | 2 ,, ........ | 10 ,, |
| Mc.Dougall's Powder .. | 12 ,, ........ | 19 ,, |
| Chloride of Lime .... | 14 ,, ........ | 21 ,, |
| Burnett's Fluid ...... | 19 ,, | |
| Carbolic Acid ........ | not tainted .... | dried up. |

A few remarks may be made on practical disinfection.

In the **Chambers of the Sick,** the atmosphere of the room has specially to be dealt with, and hence a diffusible disinfectant, such as Chlorine, Iodine, or the vapour of Carbolic Acid, will be selected   Assuming that the spread of infectious diseases depends upon the emanation of disease germs, and that the air is at least one means of their transmission, it must be remembered that whilst Chlorine and Iodine destroy the products, they do not destroy the producer, and that Carbolic Acid performs the latter, but not the former part, having therefore little power as a deodoriser, but operating on the essential cause.  The air may be carbolized by suspending in the room cloths dipped in the acid, sprinkling the floor with it, or by a spray instrument.  The vaporiser introduced by Savory and Moore is an excellent method of Carbolic Acid diffusion.  This instrument consists essentially of a metallic plate, heated by a spirit lamp, or other means, over which is suspended a glass vessel containing liquid Carbolic Acid, which falls regularly through a dropping tube, on the heated plate, drop by drop, and is dissipated in vapour. Siegle's Spray-Producer is also an useful instrument for this purpose.  The method of using Chlorine and Iodine has been previously described.  If recourse is had to the fixed disinfectants, Condy's Fluid, &c., a considerable surface of the liquid should be exposed, and this is best effected by keeping suspended cloths continually wetted with the liquid.  To fulfil the same object, Condy's Fluid, mixed with water, may be distributed through the room by means of the spray, or Siegle's apparatus.  A plan suggested by Mr. Condy is to add a wineglass-full of his red fluid to a quart of water; mix thoroughly with a teaspoonful of oil of vitriol, and then drive air through the mixture with a pair of bellows, or other special contrivance.

**Empty Rooms, Uninhabited Places, &c.,** may be most efficiently disinfected in the following manner :— The room, after infectious disease, is to be denuded of all its furniture, which should be washed with strong Chloralum solution (2½oz. to a gallon of water). Wash the floor and woodwork with soap and diluted fluid, Carbolic Acid (1 part Calvert's No. 5 to 60 of water), or Calvert's Carbolic Soap; and remove the paper, after having been treated in a similar manner with either of the liquids, for the protection of the workmen. Close up all openings, and having generated Sulphur, or Nitrous fumes, leave the room, and shut the door. Keep the apartment closed for 24 hours; then open the windows and doors, and in a few days the whitewashing and papering may be commenced. The Sulphur fumes may be generated by burning that substance in a pipkin, containing a few hot coals or otherwise, in the proportion of 4 oz. to every 100 C.F. capacity of the room.

**Bedding, Clothing, &c.,** are best disinfected by dry heat at or about 220°. If this is not practicable, before removal they should be plunged into a disinfecting solution, of no great strength, for fear of bleaching or staining in the case of the chlorides and Condy's Fluid, and then be subjected to careful washing. Dr. Sansom suggests the use of Carbolic Acid for this purpose, by placing some hot sand, or heated bricks, at the bottom of a box, and sprinkling the acid over them; the materials are then introduced layer by layer, and the box firmly closed.

**For the Disinfection of Urinals, Drains, Middens, or Sewers,** Carbolic Acid (1lb. of Calvert's No. 5, with 10 gallons of water), Chloralum, Charcoal, &c., are suitable. To remove the odour and danger of alvine discharges, Condy's Fluid (a teaspoonful to a wineglass-full of water), Sulphate of Iron, or Sulphate of Zinc (1 to 10 water), Calvert's or Mc.Dougall's Powders (¼oz. to each evacuation), Chloralum, Burnett's Fluid, &c., may be used with advantage.

**Heaps of Manure, and other Filth,** which it may at the time be impracticable to remove, or earth near dwellings, which, by the soaking of animal or vegetable matter, has become offensive, should be well watered with a solution of one of the preceding, or covered to the depth of 2 or 3 inches with freshly-burnt vegetable charcoal, in powder.

On all occasions, in the use of disinfectants, care must be taken that they are not incompatible, so as to neutralize each other. Condy's Fluid, Carbolic Acid, and Chlorine have all been used at the same time, and the only result being the destruction of the influence of each. Disinfectants, properly and judiciously applied, admit of extensive use in sanitary medicine ; their advantages, nevertheless, are not to be overrated. These agents are not *substitutes* for ventilation and cleanliness ; in fact, if no other preventive methods are adopted, they may be worse than useless, by leading to a confidence which the experience of their use does not justify. The atmosphere has chemical and physical properties which enable a state of purity to be maintained by the destruction of noxious matter introduced into it; and being always endowed with this power, the importance of a continuous and abundant supply to the chambers of the sick is evident. The oxidation destroys, and the diffusion dilutes, the noxious matters, it may be to a harmless degree, whilst the movements aid, mechanically, the entire removal of that which is injurious. But whilst these natural changes may receive important assistance from disinfectants, the latter can only be looked upon as adjuncts to ventilation. If that is neglected, their influence alone as a security against infection and disease is not to be relied upon.

**Hygiene of the Sick Room.**—The most essential requirements in the chambers of the sick are an abundance of fresh air, which is obtained more freely when the room is large, the greatest attention to ventilation, and a fireplace which, if not in use, should be kept open. Light, unless under peculiar circumstances, should be freely admitted. Both the body of the patient and the apartment should be kept very clean, and all noise and confusion around the bed is to be sedulously avoided. As an additional precaution, in cases of infectious diseases, the patient should be isolated as far as possible, and no one should enter the room save those engaged in attendance. Disinfectants should be employed in the manner which has been mentioned. As such affections may be disseminated by the excreta, as well as by the clothes, bedding, &c., additional precautions are to be used in reference to them. There should be as little furniture as possible in the room, and curtains, carpets, &c., should be removed. The vessels receiving the dejecta, saliva, &c., of the patient should contain some Condy's Fluid, Burnett's Fluid, or Chloralum, and these, with slops of all kinds, should be speedily removed from the sick chamber. The linen, &c., removed from the patient, before being taken out of the apartment, should be immersed in Condy's Fluid, a solution of Chloralum, or Carbolic Acid, or in the following mixture :—Dissolve in a tub, containing 8 gallons of cold water, 1 lb. of Hyposulphite of Soda. Into this solution plunge the articles, and, when they are saturated, add *cautiously* ¼ pint Sulphuric Acid, *previously diluted with a gallon of water*, stir, and allow the clothes to soak for an hour ; wring, rinse well three times in cold water, and dry. Instead of handkerchiefs, the patient may use rags, which should afterwards be burnt. It is well to hang a sheet, moistened with Carbolic Acid, or Condy's fluid, in the passage leading to the room. The attendants should so place themselves, that the air entering the apartment may pass from them to the patient. A vessel, containing Iodine, may be placed in the room, or a little Carbolic Acid occasionally vaporised ; or half a pound of the acid should be mixed with 10 lbs. of wet sand, placed on shallow vessels in various parts of the sick room, and renewed when its odour has disappeared. All drains, privies, and foul places, such as stables, yards, &c., should be disinfected. Let sunlight and fresh air purify every place ; open and dry all cellars, &c. Keep the grounds about dwellings dry and clean, and let personal and domestic cleanliness be everywhere observed.

These directions may be thought needlessly minute, but if by such means an insidious and unseen foe can be overcome, they are well worth the trouble demanded in the performance of them. Although it is certainly true that it is impossible to secure entire immunity from infection by any means which are at present in our possession, yet by the careful and judicious employment of methods which are available, very much can be done to diminish the risk of contagion, as well as the extension of epidemic disease.

# THE IMPURITIES OF WATER,

### AND

# THEIR REMOVAL.

---

**Importance of Pure Water for Dietetic Purposes.**—The quantity of water taken by an adult in twenty-four hours, for drinking purposes, is, on an average, about half an ounce for each pound weight of the body. A man, therefore, weighing 140 lbs. will take 70 ozs. daily, and of this quantity about 50 ozs. are taken as drink, the remainder being taken in the food. For the maintenance of perfect health, it is absolutely necessary that the water should be pure. Bad, or impure, water is the cause of a large class of diseases, and facts are abundant which go to prove that a large per centage of the cases of Typhoid fever, Cholera, Dysentery, and the like, comprehended under the term Zymotic diseases, are directly referable to the use of water rendered impure by pollution with the evacuations passed in these diseases; and, moreover, in the absence of such special causes, that simple diarrhœa, and other disorders, may be caused by the presence of animal or vegetable refuse, either in solution or suspension. These circumstances are sufficient to show the necessity of attention to any possible impurity of water by agencies of this kind. But, as Mr. Simon judiciously observes, we cannot expect to find the effect of impure water always sudden and violent; on the contrary, its results are more

usually gradual, or may elude ordinary observation, yet
be not less real and appreciable on a close enquiry. In
fact, it is only when striking and violent effects are produced that public attention is arrested; the minor and
more insidious, but not less certain, evils being suffered
with the usual indifference. The conclusion is borne out
that as precise investigations proceed, and in proportion
to the care with which the enquiry is conducted, a continually increasing class of cases is found to be connected
with the use of contaminated water; and it therefore
seems only reasonable to infer, that a still more rigid
enquiry will further prove the frequency and importance
of this mode of origin of certain diseases.

**The Causes and Effects of Water Contamina-
tion.**—The organic matter occasionally present in water
is of the first importance, and is of two kinds—Animal
and Vegetable. This consists of the remains and excreta of animal and vegetable substances, or, more
frequently, of the products of their decay and decomposition, changes which are accelerated by heat and exposure
to light. Stagnation is also favorable to putrefactive
action, whilst motion retards it, or rather, perhaps, by
facilitating oxidation, resolves the matter into its ultimate
and harmless products. These circumstances explain the
difference, in this respect, between stagnant water and
running streams. Vegetable organic matter, derived from
the soil by percolation, is present in all water; and
occasionally when it has permeated soil highly charged
with vegetable matter, the water becomes of a yellow or
brown colour, and may hold as much as 30 grains per

gallon in solution or suspension Foreign matter of this kind is not usually of great sanatory importance.

Organic matter of animal origin is also found in water. This impurity originates from the habitations of man and animals, manufactures of various kinds, and animal decomposition. These sources of pollution in a water supply are at once apparent, but there are others which are often not discovered until some bad effects have followed the use of the water. The contents of cesspools, or sewers, drain into wells, or are conducted into rivers, or the water percolates through soil more or less impregnated with decaying matters, &c., becomes charged with them, and produces effects injurious to health. Causes like these have a very extensive operation, for it is to be remembered that a well drains an extent of ground around it, in the shape of an inverted cone, which is in proportion to its own depth, and the looseness of the soil. In porous soils, a well 60 or 80 feet deep will drain an area of perhaps 200 feet in diameter. Here, then, a wide source of contamination is established for shallow wells, for by these means they may be, and very frequently are, rendered impure by sewage or sewage gas, the drainings of farm-yards, &c., and matters of all kinds thrown on the ground oozing or being washed into them. It is true that, to a certain extent, the soil through which these substances pass will filter and purify the water; but after a time that power is lost, and, finally, a channel may be formed, through which a stream of deleterious liquid is suddenly poured into a well. The insidious character of contaminations of this character is increased by the fact that many of these dissolved animal substances give no taste or smell to the water unless they are in large quantities, or unless ammonia, sulphuretted hydrogen, or other fetid gases are present; and it may even be, and often is, cool, sparkling, and agreeable in flavour. Leaving out of consideration the question whether organic matter in solution or in suspension is the more dangerous to health, it is certain that a larger amount is dissolved when the weather is warm than when it is cold, and it is highly probable that, under certain conditions, not well defined, the matter may undergo putrefactive changes which render it suddenly and directly poisonous: and there can be no doubt that habitually drinking water of this kind is not only capable of producing certain disorders, but has a tendency to act as a predisposing cause of disease.

**Relation of Typhoid Fever and Impure Water.**— Modern science has shown that certain epidemic diseases, such as some forms of fever, cholera, &c., are the result of a specific poison introduced into the human system. Whatever may be its precise character, whether germ or otherwise, the evidence is irresistible that it may, through the medium of water, be introduced into the system, and establish the special disease. Sir W. Jenner says, " The spread of typhoid fever is, if possible, less disputable than the spread of cholera by the same means. Solitary cases, outbreaks confined to single houses, to small villages, and to parts of large towns—cases isolated, it seems, from all sources of fallacy—and epidemics, affecting the inhabitants of large though limited localities, have all united to support by their testimony the truth of the opinion that the admixture of a trace of fecal matter, but especially the bowel-excreta of typhoid fever, with the water supplied for drinking purposes, is the most efficient cause of the spread of the disease; and that the diffusion of the disease, in any given locality, is limited, or otherwise, and just in proportion as the dwellers of that locality derive their supply of drinking water from polluted sources."

No better illustration can be given of the truth and importance of these considerations than the outbreaks of fever which occurred at Ackworth School and Bramham College, as reported in the *British Medical Journal*, by Dr. Clifford Allbutt. In March, 1870, typhoid fever broke out at Ackworth School and Ackworth Moor top, near Pontefract. The school was supplied with water from two sources—one at the Institution; the other at the village; and the latter was the source from which the water used at the school was chiefly obtained, which was also the case at Ackworth Moor top. It was clear and sparkling, agreeable in flavour, and gave, on analysis, rather more than five grains of organic matter, with six of chloride of sodium to the gallon, and an unusually large quantity of nitrates and nitrites. All the cases which occurred were in the area supplied by this water, except that of one boy, who passed the well twice daily, and frequently drank the water. A careful examination of the locality revealed the fact that the water was impregnated with sewage matter, draining from some cottages, and the first case of fever was that of a girl, who was brought home suffering from the disease, from Wakefield, to one of the dwellings, and was thus the means of introducing the poisonous matter.

The other instance occurred at Bramham College, near Tadcaster. In the latter part of March, 1869, nineteen boys were, at or about the same time, attacked with typhoid fever. This sudden irruption showed that there must have been a common cause in operation. The village was supplied with water from a well; the water had a pleasant taste, but, on analysis, gave evidence of sewage admixture. Adjoining the well was a soft water tank, which was cemented on the inside. On the side of it, next the well, the cement was found to be shelling off, and oozing was going on from the tank into the well; and it was, moreover, discovered that the tank water was contaminated with sewage matter, derived from a drain passing over the top of the tank, from a water closet, to a sewage reservoir; cracks were detected in the pipes composing it, through which the matter dropped into the tank. The introduction of the specific poison was readily explained. In February, two boys were attacked with the fever, and circumstances showed that the infection had been imbibed before their arrival at Bramham, and that in this manner, through the agency of the water, the disease had been introduced into the school.

As Dr. C. Allbutt remarks, in both these cases, it is worthy of notice, that so far as enteric fever was concerned, the water had been drunk with impunity, until, with sewage matter, the fever poison passed into it.

Dr. Buchanan had to investigate an outbreak of fever in a village in Essex. There were eleven wells in the village, and he found that out of the 45 cases of fever, among a population of 200, 42 had drunk of one particular well. All the wells had been equally affected by the sinking of the soil water, but the one in question happened to be only 35 yards distant from the privy into which the stools of the first indigenous case had been thrown without previous disinfection.

**The Relation of Water to Cholera Poisoning** is equally interesting, although the connection seems to have been overlooked by the earlier investigators of this disease, in 1849.

Dr. Snow, whilst investigating some outbreaks of cholera, the limits of which were circumscribed, came to the conclusion that in these instances the disease was attributable to cholera evacuations finding their way into the drinking water. Gradually fresh instances were collected, and, in 1854, occurred the celebrated instance of the Broad-street pump, which was investigated by a committee, who were perfectly convinced that, in that instance at least, the poison of cholera had found its way into the body by means of the drinking water. In July, 1854, an outbreak of cholera occurred in the parish of St. James, Westminster. From the 31st August to the 8th September, there occurred 486 fatal cases in a small area marked off by a circle whose radius would be 210 yards. Such a phenomenon as this was unusual in our English experience of cholera, and led Dr. Snow to hope that an investigation of this outbreak might throw fresh light on the whole system of cholera propagation. Fixing his attention steadily on the local peculiarities of the district, Dr. Snow

D

quickly perceived that one remarkable circumstance was common to the history of the large majority of attacks of the disease, viz., that the sufferers had been in the habit of drinking the water of a well, in Broad-street, which had a great reputation for sweetness and freshness. Analysis of this water soon showed that it was highly charged with organic impurities, and, on the 8th September, the vestry, on the urgent persuasion of Dr. Snow, removed the handle of the pump, and so prevented the further use of the well. The disease then gradually declined, and ultimately ceased. On subsequent examination, it was discovered that the sewage from a neighbouring house drain had leaked into the well, and it was moreover shown that the discharges of a patient residing in the house in question, and suffering from severe diarrhœa, if not from actual cholera, must have mingled with the sewage immediately before the date of the great epidemic outbreak. The history of this epidemic, taken in connection with analagous but less striking facts which had been before observed, afforded strong presumption, if not proof, of the important part which impure drinking-water might play in the propagation of cholera, acting at least as one of its means of dissemination. The matter was not allowed to rest here. An examination of the circumstances of cholera development amongst the inmates of the houses supplied with water by the Lambeth and Southwark companies respectively, displayed the remarkable fact that the ratio of mortality was three-and-a-half times greater in the former instance than in the latter; and an analysis of the water of the two companies showed a corresponding difference from organic impurities. There are instances of this kind, where towns which have suffered severely in one epidemic have escaped a later one, which can only be explained by the fact that in the interval the supply of water has improved. Exeter, Hull, Newcastle-on-Tyne, and Glasgow, are instances of this kind. Numerous other illustrations of a direct and indirect character might be brought forward in support of the opinion expressed on this point, but it is by no means intended to be held that water is the *only* means by which the disease can be communicated.

**General Considerations.**—Leaving out of the question the presence of a specific disease poison, the evidence is irresistible that the existence of organic matter in water is an exciting and predisposing cause of disease. It is difficult to state the quantity which may be deemed harmless. The general tendency of opinion has been to regard the presence of organic matter as decidedly objectionable when the quantity exceeds two grains per gallon, which is only $\frac{1}{35000}$ by weight. But the nature and condition are of more importance than the amount, that condition being in relation to its activity, or disposition to undergo fermentation, or putrefactive changes. Then it is the most pernicious. With this there will have to be taken into account the presence or absence of other constituents, or conditions, which may assist, accelerate, or retard these decompositions. Dr. A. Smith says :—" Water, for example, may contain the juices of plants of a wholesome character. If these juices are fresh, they do no injury, but they soon putrefy. Water containing organic matter ready to putrefy ought to be avoided, as we cannot tell when the moment of danger begins ; whilst the quality at best is never known to us exactly." One result of the decomposition of organic matter (in the presence of alkaline, or earthy salts) is the formation of **Nitrates and Nitrites.** These salts do not appear to be found in water when decomposition is going on very rapidly. In the most impure condition of the Thames, scarcely any nitrates were detectible in the water. All the conditions requisite for their formation are not known, but it is essential that oxygen shall be present. Their presence is in itself of no importance as indicating the quality of the water, for they are the result of a change of a purifying character, and have no longer any influence on the water in a sanitary point of view. It is, in fact, evidence that the organic impurity has been converted into harmless products. But, on the other hand, their presence indicates that the water *has been the subject of contamination*, and there is no certainty that the whole of it has undergone change ; also, there remains the possibility that the water now pure may again become impure from the causes previously in operation.

Dr. Frankland considers the estimation of these (nitrogenous) substances of the highest importance, as he regards them as indicative of " previous sewage contamination." All chemists do not accept this opinion. Dr. Letheby even asserts that a flow of 10 or 12 miles in a river is sufficient to counteract the contamination of water with 5 per cent. its bulk of sewage matter, and render it wholesome. But, again, this statement has not received

general assent, although it is admitted that such circumstances have great influence in purifying water which is
contaminated. When nitrates or nitrites are present,
they certainly indicate that an equivalent of albuminous
or sewage matter *has* existed ; and assuming that their
origin can be traced to no local source, they must be
looked upon as being derived from an albuminous form of
organic matter, in which the process of oxidation (in this
sense synonymous with destruction) may, or may not be,
completed.

Another constituent of water, in relation to organic
matter, is **Common Salt (Chloride of Sodium)**,
which Dr. Angus Smith takes as the index of animal contamination, and accordingly attaches great importance
to its presence and quantity. It remains after animal
decomposition, and, consequently, exists largely in the
drainage of grave yards, sewers, &c. In forming an
opinion of the character of a water from the presence of
chlorides, care must be exercised, as they may occur from
many causes besides the existence of organic matter ; and
their origin will, therefore, demand careful and minute
enquiry, and a comparison will have to be made between
this water and the water of the district. But in all cases,
if any large amount is present, the water should not be
used for dietetic purposes without a searching investigation
into their origin.

. METHODS OF DETECTING THE IMPURITIES IN WATER.

*(1)* **Physical Examination.**—In endeavouring to
ascertain the goodness or badness of water, the informa-

tion derived from a mere physical examination can by no means be relied on. Smell will detect offensive gases, if they are present, and this will be facilitated by shaking the water well in a large bottle, the hand being placed over its mouth, and by then smelling it. The colour and transparency are often, but not always, a valuable test; for while suspended matters may give a perceptible tinge of colour, or turbidity, this is no indication alone that the water is unwholesome, and, on the other hand, a water holding much organic matter in solution may be perfectly clear and colourless. Dr. Letheby places great reliance on this colour test, when a sufficient depth of water is used. He advises it to be practised, by looking through the liquid contained in a tall glass, two feet high and one inch in diameter, placed on a white plate, or piece of paper, by which means more minute changes of colour are detected; and, for a comparison, another similar glass vessel is filled with distilled water. If organic matter is present, the water has usually a shade of yellow, green, or blue; but in forming an opinion from these indications, it is to be remembered that the presence of some other substances, such as iron, &c., will produce similar alterations of colour.

The Microscope is a valuable aid in the examination of water. After standing twelve or sixteen hours, the sediment may be examined microscopically, and if the liquid has been very impure, evidence of animal or vegetable life, or their *debris*, will be detected under the form of parts of their several structures, and different species of Infusoria, &c. (Paramecia, Diatoms, Ento-

mostraca, &c.), may be seen. If, under these circumstances, no evidence is furnished, the water in a flask,
having the neck plugged with cotton wool, to exclude
atmospheric contamination, should be freely exposed to
light for a day or two, for the development of all possible
germs. These will then be detected by the microscope, or
green (Confervoid) matter show itself in quantity pro-
portional to the impurity. This mode of investigation is
of the highest value to the sanitarian, for by it he is
enabled readily to ascertain whether active matter is
present, on which, in a great measure, the injurious or
harmless character of the impurity in water depends.

(2) **Chemical Examination.**—The information, then,
that is gained by the mere physical examination of water,
is, alone, neither of a very exact nor accurate character;
yet it is most essential that we should be in possession of
means by which the presence of animal or vegetable
impurities can be readily and easily detected when they
exist in such quantity that the use of the water containing
them may be prejudicial to health. Such means are well
known to chemists, and in this, as a popular treatise, it is
proposed to mention a few methods, without critical dis-
cussion of their defects or merits, which may, with a little
practice, be employed by any person, and give a good
general idea of the quality of water under examination.
The estimation of the *exact quantity* of organic impregnation is a difficult problem of science, which can only be
undertaken by the experienced analyst.

Formerly, the method of determining the amount of
organic matter was by **incineration**. A pint or so of the

water was evaporated to dryness in a water-bath, and the residue incinerated at as low a heat as possible, to destroy the organic matter, the loss of weight before and after incineration being considered to represent the quantity originally present in the water. Although this method is full of fallacies, useful information respecting the character of the water may be gathered from it, especially by the colour of the ash, which will be, more or less, black, according to the quantity of organic matter present. The presence of the nitrates will be indicated by the deflagration of the residue. Often during the evaporation, if albuminous matter exists, it is coagulated by the heat, and falls in stringy or flocculent masses.

Organic impregnation may be detected by boiling 6 or 8 ounces of the water with a few drops of a solution of Chloride of Gold. In proportion to the quantity of organic matter, the gold is reduced, and falls as a violet or black powder.

Mr. Heisch, about two years since, proposed a method for the detection of sewage matter which had the merit of extreme simplicity. He proposed to place some of the water to be examined in a flask, with a small quantity of sugar. This was then exposed to light, at a moderate temperature. ˙ If organic matter was present, in the course of a few hours, a peculiar odour was developed, the liquid became more or less opaque, and fungi were eventually developed in it. But Dr. Frankland has shown, that in order to produce these changes, the presence of organic matter is not essential, and that the same phenomena occur in any water which contains phosphates. Hence, for the purpose for which it was introduced, it is not to be relied on, but may be used as a corroborative test.

Dr. Burdon Sanderson, from experiments which he has made, arrives at the conclusion that water is the primary source from whence Bacteria, infinitely minute elongated bodies, probably of animal nature (Vibriones) are derived. Since their development in water depends upon the presence of nitrogen, they are, therefore, associated with a condition of impurity. It thus follows that the greater the amount of this impurity, the more abundantly are these bodies developed. On these facts is based the " Zymotic Test" for the impurity of water. A small cylindrical glass, capable of holding about three drachms, is first heated to 395°F. This is then half filled with boiling Pasteur's solution (which is a solution of sugar, tartrate of ammonia, and yeast ash), and to this are added five drops of the water to be tested, the mouth of the glass being plugged with cotton wool. If impure, after the lapse of from 6 to 10 days, the upper part of the liquid will be observed to be opalescent, and, on examination with the microscope, Bacteria (microzymes) will be detected. The amount of impurity is measured by the degree of opacity. The tube in which the water is collected must previously be heated to a high degree, and in that state sealed hermetically; it is filled by breaking off one end whilst it is under the water.

The most simple and readily applied test depends upon the fact that the colour of a certain solution is destroyed when added to water containing organic matter. The test is performed in the following manner :—A weak solution is made of **Permanganate of Potash** ; or Condy's (crimson) fluid, which is a similar solution, is diluted— either of them is the test solution. Take half a pint or more of the water to be examined, previously acidified by the addition of a few drops of hydrochloric (muriatic) acid, or about 12 drops of sulphuric acid (oil of vitriol) diluted with five parts of water, add the test solution, drop by drop, whilst stirring, until a faint pink tinge is perceptible. Every fifteen minutes the water is to be looked at, and as the colour disappears, a few drops more of the test solution cautiously added, and this is to be so continued until the colour remains permanent for half an hour. All the organic matter is then destroyed (oxidised), and the quantity of solution required to effect this gives a rough estimate of the matter originally in the water. The change of colour is better observed by placing the vessel upon a sheet of white paper before a window, and looking down at the paper through the liquid.

If the solutions are accurately prepared, and the process conducted carefully, the exact quantity of (oxidisable) organic matter can be estimated, and an opinion formed of the fitness of the water for dietetic purposes. Although the operation is a delicate one, the estimation may be made with some degree of accuracy by the following method :—Dissolve two grains of pure Permanganate of Potash in rather more than half a pint (10¼ oz.) of distilled water; ten minims of this solution yield $\frac{1}{1000}$ of a grain of oxygen. Fill an apothecary's minim measure with this solution, and proceed with a known quantity of water in the manner previously described; and then read from the marks on the glass the quantity which has been required to produce discoloration, and dividing this by ten, the result gives the number of thousandths of grains of oxygen consumed. In the case of the London water, the amount of oxygen required varies from $\frac{1}{4000}$ to $\frac{1}{1200}$ of a grain per gallon, and the quantity of organic matter is about eight times this quantity.

In judging of the indications afforded by this test, it is to be remembered that *putrid* organic matter, and its gaseous products, *rapidly* effect decoloration, whilst that which is more recent produces the same result much more slowly. To this fact Dr. Angus Smith attaches great importance, as giving some insight into the condition of the impurity. Hence, in using this test, the quantity decomposed *instantly* should be carefully noted, and taken to indicate the amount of putrid matter, unless Nitrites are present, which produce a similar effect ; while the quantity which decolorises slowly is indicative of more recent, less decomposable (oxidizable), and probably less injurious organic matter.

This permanganate test is open to numerous objections, but although it does not supply all the demands of the chemist, it is, in general, sufficient for sanitary purposes. Iron acts on it in a similar manner to organic matter. The gases of decomposition, and other bodies not organic, as the nitrites, bleach the permanganate, but the presence of these substances is revealed by their appropriate tests. Although, then, it is true, as Dr. Miller remarks, that this colour method is liable to these defects, yet the same objection applies to other processes. And, further, it is in the highest degree probable that the substances most readily oxidised are those most likely to be injurious in their effects upon those who drink the water. Practically, therefore, it admits of very ready and useful application, especially when a thorough examination is impracticable, and the great object is to ascertain whether the water is bad or tolerably good, and justifies the inference that if decoloration is effected, the water is to be regarded with suspicion.

**Detection of Nitrogenous Matter.**—It is a prevalent idea that the deleterious influence of organic substances on the water is confined to the portions more liable to putrefaction containing nitrogen (nitrogenised or azotised substances), and giving among the results of that putrefaction, ammonia, nitrates, and nitrites, and, therefore, that the determination of the amount of nitrogen would be an index to the degree of contamination of the water. On this principle a method has been devised by **Dr. Frankland,** by which he estimates the amount of organic carbon in the dissolved contents, the total amount of combined nitrogen, and that existing as ammonia, &c. The difference between the two last data gives the amount of nitrogen existing in the organic substance of the water, and this is taken to be the measure of the quality of the water in reference to the organic matter. It is one, doubtless, of the highest value, but too elaborate for description in this place.

Another method, on a somewhat similar basis, has been proposed by **Messrs. Wanklyn & Chapman,** which requires for its performance some experience in chemical

manipulation. and great care in the matter of clean
vessels. &c. Mr. Wanklyn proposes. in the first instance.
to remove the ammonia, which exists as such in the
water. by boiling with carbonate of soda, and then to
decompose any urea, albumen, or like nitrogenous
matter which may be present, with permanganate of
potash, and boiling with potash ; ammonia, the result of
the latter decomposition, is obtained, and may be detected by the addition of Nessler's test, which gives a
yellow or brown tinge, or precipitate, according to the
quantity present. A pint and a half of the water is
mixed with 30 grains of carbonate of soda, and rapidly
distilled in separate portions until it gives no reaction
with Nessler's test. The residue is then distilled with
5 grains of permanganate of potash, and caustic potash,
and the ammonia comes over, and is tested as before.
This latter is taken as " Albuminoid Ammonia," whilst
the quantity obtained by the distillation with the soda, is
called " Free Ammonia." Conducted carefully, and with
attention to the absence of ammonia from other sources,
this is an excellent and simple test for the presence of
(nitrogenised) organic matter, and is the one now generally
adopted. The determination of the quantity, which is
taken as a measure of the deleterious substance in the
water, is a more delicate operation, and is effected from a
solution of ammonia of known strength, by adding to it, and
an equal volume of the distilled liquid, a given quantity
of Nessler's test, and repeating this comparative observation with different quantities of ammonia until the tint of
the standard solution coincides with that of the distillate.

**The Presence of the Nitrates or Nitrites** may be detected in water by the deflagration of the residue, left on evaporation when it is ignited. Indication of the nitrates will also be afforded by the following tests, after evaporating a pint of water to a very small bulk :—

(1) Pour a portion into a test-tube, and add the same quantity of pure sulphuric acid, so that it may form a layer under the water. When cool, drop in a crystal of sulphate of iron. A dark olive-green ring will be formed at the junction of the two liquids if Nitrates are present.

(2) To the concentrated water, a few drops of sulphuric acid and indigo are added; when warmed, the presence of nitrates is shown by the disappearance of the blue colour.

(8) The presence of one part of Nitric Acid in 1,000 parts of water may be detected as recommended by Kersting. To about 20 drops of the water, in a small test-tube, add the same quantity of a saturated aqueous solution of Brucine; then, by means of a pipeth, send a few drops of pure sulphuric acid to the bottom of the tube. If nitric acid is present, a pink zone will appear at the junction of the two liquids, turning yellow before it disappears.

Mr. Nicholson says a much more delicate method of applying the test is to evaporate the water, and add a few drops of sulphuric acid, a fragment of Brucine is then dropped in, and moved about with a fine glass point.

**For the Detection of Nitrites,** the water is evaporated as before, and to it is added a clear mixture, made of 1 part iodide of potassium, 20 of starch, and 500 of boiling water, with a little acetic acid; an indigo blue tint indicates the presence of nitrites.

**Chlorides.**—The importance and significance of the Chlorides in water has been mentioned as an indication of sewage contamination. But it must not be forgotten that innocuous sources of Chlorides exist—(1) By the sea spray, which may find its way far inland to the water-bearing strata; and, (2) By the occurrence of saliferous rocks, or springs. The amount of chlorine in the Thames water supplied in London is less than one and a half grain per gallon, while in London sewage about 7 grains per gallon occur. The presence of compounds of chlorine can be ascertained by adding a few drops of nitric acid to the water, and then a solution of nitrate of silver, when, if they exist, a white precipitate falls, which, in the presence of organic matter, is more or less dark coloured. With this test, 4 grains of chloride of sodium (common salt) per gallon gives a turbidity; 10 grains, a slight precipitate; and 20 grains, a considerable precipitate; so that a guess can thus be made of the quantity present.

**Hard and Soft Water.**—So far, attention has been directed to the constitution of water in reference to its fitness for dietetic purposes, but it will not be inopportune to make a few remarks on the inorganic, or saline, con-tituents, which are, in a chemical sense, impurities, and affect the value of the water for many economic uses. Water which contains only a small amount of saline matter in solution, or when this consists mainly of alkaline (potash and soda) salts, is called *soft*. Such water dissolves soap, with scarcely any change. Whilst water holding salts of lime, magnesia, or iron, in solution, is called *hard*, and decomposes or curdles soap. The so-called "hardness" is due chiefly to the carbonates, sulphates, and chlorides of calcium (lime), and magnesium. The carbonates are held in solution by the gas carbonic acid, and when the water is boiled, this gas, by which the solution is effected, being driven off, they are precipitated. The production of "fur" in kettles and boilers, &c., is the result of this action. By the removal of the carbonates in this manner, the remaining water is rendered softer, but it may, according to the original composition, still retain an amount of (permanent) hardness due to the matter (sulphates and chlorides) not precipitated. It is on the same principle that water, the hardness of which is due to carbonate of lime, is softened by the addition of lime. The former substance is removed by precipitation, carrying down with it suspended matters, as well as the more organised organic matter, if it is present, and leaving behind that portion which, in a sanitary point of view, is of less consequence. The action of soda, in softening water for washing, tea-making, &c., is of a similar kind.

**Characters of Good Water.**—We are now in a position to consider the qualities which good potable water should possess. Dr. Parkes gives the following as the essential characters in relation to the dissolved constituents. Organic matter should not exceed one-and-a-half grain per gallon ; carbonate of lime, 16 grains ; sulphate of lime, 8 grains ; carbonate and sulphate of magnesia, 3 grains; chloride of sodium, 10 grains; carbonate of soda, 20 grains; sulphate of soda, 6 grains; and the total solid contents should not exceed' 35 grains per gallon.

It is a prevalent opinion that the less the quantity of saline matter in water, the better it is adapted for drinking purposes; but, on the whole, the evidence would go to show that the existence of this matter in moderate quantity does not deteriorate the quality of the water, and it would be ridiculous to attempt to lay down a fixed standard, as that must be dependent upon so many varying circumstances. Whatever difference of opinion may be entertained respecting the dietetic value of hard water, for culinary, washing, and most manufacturing purposes, the presence of saline matter is decidedly objectionable. Hard water is a less perfect solvent of organic matter than soft water, and is therefore inferior for boiling, making tea, and cooking. In proportion to the hardness, more soap is used in washing, for it has to overcome that hardness before it can exert any detergent properties, on account of the fatty acids of the soap forming insoluble compounds (becoming curdled) with the mineral ingredients of the water.

**Contamination with Lead.**—Water is occasionally liable to be contaminated by contact with Lead, and as this metal is largely used for water-cisterns and pipes, the possibility of this taking place is frequent. The quantity which may prove injurious is often very small. From cases which have occurred, it seems probable that the habitual use of water containing ₁/₇ to ₁/₅ grain per

E

gallon may be dangerous. In fact, all lead contamination of water is to be looked upon with the gravest suspicion as liable to set up general disorder of the system, especially of the alimentary canal and digestive organs, or even to produce lead colic, paralysis, &c. The action of water on lead will depend entirely upon its chemical constitution, and although there is in detail some difference of opinion on the subject, we are, nevertheless, acquainted with the conditions under which the metal does, or does not, become dissolved. The water most liable to become poisoned by contact with lead is that which contains little (less than $\frac{1}{15000}$ part) or no saline matter, as in rain and very soft water, and this is facilitated by the presence of organic matters, and the more so if nitrates and nitrites are likewise present. The hard waters do not usually exercise any solvent action, since the effect of the carbonate and sulphate of lime is to produce an *insoluble* coating of lead salts on the interior of the pipes, which acts the part of a protective varnish, and prevents further action, but it is true that a large quantity of carbonic acid in the water may dissolve this when it has been produced by carbonates alone. The presence of $\frac{1}{5000}$ of its weight of sulphate of lime in water entirely prevents lead contamination. Junction with pipes of a different metal facilitates the action of water on those made of lead, by establishing galvanic action. To prevent poisoning of this kind, the lead is often covered with a coating of various substances, such as tin, bitumens, some resins, &c. The use of iron pipes and cisterns, of course, entirely prevents the mischief, and is, in a large number of cases, desirable, if only as a precautionary measure. Lead may be readily detected by evaporating, to a small bulk, 6 or 8 pints of the suspected water, previously acidified with nitric acid, when, if this metal is present, the addition of sulphuretted hydrogen will darken the liquid.

**Removal of Impurities from Water.**—Reverting to the consideration of organic matter, and assuming its presence in water, the practical questions are—Can such matter be removed or destroyed ? And to what extent, and by what means can this be effected ?

Experience teaches that it is rather the *quality* than the *quantity* of organic matter which determines the dangerous character of water ; and if it be true, as modern science has almost demonstrated, that the real agents of such diseases as infectious fevers, cholera, rinderpest, and other allied (zymotic) affections are living germs, and not a gas, or vapour, or dead organic matter, it becomes a physiological, rather than a chemical question, to decide on the means best fitted for their destruction. That which has been proved in respect of small-pox and other allied diseases, is very applicable to the present enquiry, so far as it relates to the most probable existence of germs in the water we may drink. The agents, then, of these diseases, it is believed, are living germs, capable of remaining dormant for an uncertain, but not indefinite, time, and then springing into activity when they find the conditions requisite for their development. But whether these germs are capable of destruction by oxidation is an unsettled question. We do, however, know that these germs are destroyed by a high temperature, that they are

killed by a large number of caustic substances, and that
they cannot resist the action of certain agents, such as
carbolic acid, which act on them as specific poisons. Therefore to this class, rather than to oxidising agents, we look
for their removal, and in the case under consideration the
reliable agent is heat ; for if water is boiled, there is every
probability that the poisonous matter will be rendered
harmless. The destruction of decaying organic debris is
also of the greatest importance, its presence being
productive of disease. It is certain that matters of this
description are rapidly destroyed (oxidised) by permanganate of potash (Condy's fluid), and by filtration through
animal charcoal alone, or mixed with certain compounds
of iron. But it is more than doubtful, even if it were
practicable, whether such processes should be used by the
water companies at the sources of supply, having regard
to the numerous causes of pollution which exist between
these sources and the consumer. Moreover, it must not be
forgotten that only a very small part of the water delivered
by the companies is used for dietetic purposes, the bulk
being employed for flushing closets, watering streets, and
in manufacturing operations. It would, therefore, be an
unnecessary and wasteful application of a tedious and
expensive process to do that at the works which can be so
easily, and more economically, done by the consumer.
As a matter of health, too much importance cannot be
attached to a *continuous water supply.* If this were general,
among the poorer class especially, it would do away with
the prolific sources of contamination arising from the ab-
sorption of atmospheric impurities, from the filthy recep-

tacles of many kinds, and from the storing in close, badly ventilated, and crowded rooms, and often dirty cisterns. When this is not carried out, the fault does not rest entirely with the water companies, for a constant supply can scarcely be expected whilst almost every household service.is in its present imperfect condition, and the reckless waste of water is uncontrolled. Then, again, the owners of cottage property, where abundance of water is of vital importance, are unwilling to pay for it in the quantity demanded. In London, the daily water supply is about 30 gallons per head, whereas Dr. Letheby is inclined to believe that, with good regulations, mainly on the part of the consumer, it need not exceed 20 gallons.

Filtration.—In the purification of water, filtration is an important agent, but the extent to which it is efficiently secured will depend upon the material composing the filter. When water containing organic or other matter in *suspension* is made to pass through gravel, sand, loam, or other porous substance, this matter is retained, and the water passes out clear. But in the case of sand, and particularly loam, it is now known that they do more than merely remove the matter mechanically; they also take away an appreciable quantity of salts, in *solution*, to the extent of 5 to 15 per cent. of the amount originally in the water. But filters of this kind do not materially affect the organic matter with which we have especially to deal. Charcoal is capable of doing much that we require in this respect, as well as of diminishing the quantity of saline matter. When a sufficient thickness of the material is used, it is capable of removing upwards of 85 per cent. of the organic, and 25 per cent. of the mineral, matter from the water filtered through it. In this property vegetable is inferior to animal charcoal. Gaultier de Claubry states that one part of *animal charcoal* purifies 136 times its weight of very impure water; and one part of *vegetable charcoal* 116 times its weight. But if the water is moderately good, one pound will purify 60 gallons, or 600 times its weight. To effect this the charcoal should be of some thickness, and closely pressed.

After use for a certain time, both animal and vegetable charcoals lose their absorptive power, but admit of renovation by being removed from the filter, thoroughly dried, and freely exposed to the air, or more quickly by heating. A simple and effectual filter (fig 8) may be readily constructed. A wooden or zinc conical vessel is provided with two perforated shelves, *a;* over the upper one, for the formation of the space *b*, is a third shelf, *c;* through these a water-tight tube, *d*, passes, which places the upper and lower compartments in communication; from the upper compartment, *b*, a small air-tube, *e*, runs upwards. The filtering substance consists at the bottom of small pebbles, in the middle of gravel, and at the top of a layer of bone black (animal charcoal.) The water to be filtered is poured in at the top, passes through the tube *d* to the inferior compartment, and then filters up to *b*, where it collects as the air escapes through the air tube. The lowest compartment has an opening for washing out such dirt, &c., as may collect.

A simple cottage filter may be made from a common flower pot. The hole is stopped, but not too tightly, with a piece of sponge, and then filled nearly to the top with the following substances. At the bottom, a layer of charcoal, then one of clean sand, and finally covered with fine gravel. Water poured in at the top, filters through these, and passes out at the plugged hole.

Many excellent filters are manufactured, and a few may be mentioned with which the writer has a practical acquaintance. Those sent out by the Silicated Carbon Company are manufactured from the coke of the Torbane Hill Mineral, which is made into a paste with pitch, pressed into the required form, and burnt in a kiln. This block is cemented into a vessel, dividing it into two chambers, and constitutes the filtering medium. It consists of 75 per cent. carbon (charcoal), and 22 silica, with a little oxide of iron and alumina. Water passed through this filter is deprived of nearly all its organic matter, with a portion of the carbonate of lime and iron, and is left cool and transparent. It is an excellent filter, and, with a little attention, retains its properties for a very long time.

The Patent Moulded Carbon Filter is an elegant article for the side-board. It consists of a block of charcoal, into which a glass tube is inserted; this passes into a lower vessel, which receives the filtered water, and can be used at table as a water bottle. In the removal of the organic impurities it does not seem so efficient as the Silicated Carbon Filter.

The London Water Purifying Company construct a filter on Danchell's Patent. The filtering-block, which has certain assumed advantages of form, is immersed in the water, and consequently filters upwards, and is discharged on the syphon principle. It is highly satisfactory in relation to the purification effected.

Several years since Mr Spencer drew attention to the marvellous power that certain oxides of iron possessed of removing organic impurities from water, and on this principle is constructed the Magnetic Carbide Filter. The material is prepared by heating together sawdust and red iron ore (hæmatite). Whilst in relation to its filtering powers this preparation has all the good properties of charcoal, it seems to have the advantage of retaining its activity for any length of time The only possible objection is that it communicates to the water a slight taste of iron. Filters are often rendered inoperative from their pores becoming choked up with suspended material. This may, in a great measure, be obviated by making the water pass through a sponge before reaching the filtering medium. It has been remarked previously, that in all probability some kinds of organic matter are capable of resisting oxidation, and, consequently, removal by filtration. This statement derives support from the result of the experiments of Chauveau on germs, and the cause of the activity of vaccine and small-pox poisons. He says they are not decomposed in the beds of running streams, and pass unaffected through filters, but that heat has the power of destroying their vitality and breaking them up. To secure the purity of water, then, the practical conclusion is that all water, especially that stored in cisterns, or other receptacles, should be boiled before it is drunk, should be filtered through charcoal alone, or mixed with one of the oxides of iron ; and failing this, or as an additional precaution, it may be treated with a little Condy's fluid until it retains a decided pink tint.

The matters which have been discussed in the preceding pages have a most intimate association with all epidemics, and this is the case to such an extent, that, was due attention paid to sanitary considerations, in reference especially to air and water, these diseases would be classed amongst those which are preventable. In order to give an idea of the awful sacrifice of life caused by these epidemics, in a great measure the result of a disregard to the ordinary laws of health, it is sufficient simply to quote the figures afforded by the Report of the Registrar General. In the four quarters of 1871, 101,358 deaths were referred to the seven principal zymotic diseases, against 98,081 in 1870 : of these 22,907 resulted from small-pox, 9,233 from measles, 18,282 from scarlet fever, 2,405 from diptheria, 9,616 from whooping cough, 15,396 from different kinds of fever, and 23,519 from diarrhœa. Or it may be taken in another manner. In rural districts, the percentage of the total deaths is 17 from zymotic diseases; in Birmingham it is 27 ; in London and Manchester it is 25·5 ; in Leeds it is 24·5 ; and in Liverpool it is upwards of 28. As respects their causation by impure air and water, in none of these diseases is the relation more distinctly traceable than in typhoid fever. Of this fatal fever, two exciting causes are recognised as of far greater importance than all others. The first is the direct introduction of decomposing organic matters (and possibly of organic germs developed from this source) into the stomach by the agency of impure drinking water, and the second is the inhalation of the gases formed by the decomposition of organic matter, and possibly of specific germs with them. A typical illustration will show the operation of these agencies. A town disposes of its sewage in cesspools. From the latter, by reason of the nature of the soil, or on account of their close proximity, an oozing of decomposed and decomposing organic matter takes place more or less into the wells. This may go on, even for years, without particular harm; but at length there comes a long dry summer by which the water is reduced to a low level, and which concentrates and favours the decomposition of its impurities. Under such circumstances, typhoid fever becomes developed. Or, under the favouring influence of a hot dry season, sewage decomposition is increased and accelerated; the gases ascend through the imperfect traps of the drains into the interior of the houses, and frequently establish an outbreak of typhoid fever. Hence will be explained that which has been noted, that the long continuance of hot dry summer weather greatly predisposes to the occurrence of this disease, whilst, on the contrary, a cold and wet summer and autumn are opposed to its development.

The facts are numerous which lead to the conclusion, and it has been exemplified in many towns, that, by rendering the drinking water absolutely pure, and by disinfecting the sewage at the earliest moment, typhoid fever may be almost or entirely suppressed.

With regard to that group of epidemics which includes

scarlatina, measles, &c., the general unhealthiness of
dirt, impure air, foul drinking water, &c., add to the
severity of their attack, and give a strong impulse to their
propagation.

Whilst, then, it is certain that earnest action on the
part of the Legislature, in relation to the causes on which
they depend for their dissemination, would materially
diminish, if not annihilate these plagues, there are other
epidemics which demand another kind of remedy.

The history of the cotton famine in England, and of
the distresses in Ireland, shows that those conditions
were established under which were set up relapsing and
typhus fever, diseases owing their development, if not
their origin, to scarcity of food and the various social
miseries which follow in its train. Typhus is pre-
eminently a disease of the poor; it is the plague of our
large overcrowded towns, and flourishes in the courts and
alleys densely inhabited by the poorest of our population.
The causes are famine, or an insufficient supply of food,
and overcrowding, involving of necessity imperfect ventilation. As a result of this state of things, another class
of insanitary conditions is established. Poverty attends
sickness, destroys the feelings of self-respect amongst
the needy, leading them to neglect cleanliness, and thus
the foulness of their apartments is aggravated. These
diseases will have to be combated by good food, good
clothing, and a greater amount of breathing space than
is usually found in the abodes of the sufferers. The
remedies are, that the administrators of the Poor Law
exercise an unlimited extension of relief in accordance

with the demand, and the establishment in every town of a roomy, well-constructed, and thoroughly ventilated fever hospital.

In conclusion, I cannot do better than quote the following passage from the Thirteenth Report of the Medical Officer of the Privy Council :—" It seems certain that the deaths which occur in this country are fully a third more numerous than they would be if an existing knowledge of the chief causes of diseases were reasonably well applied throughout the country; that of deaths which, in this sense, may be called preventable, the average yearly number in England and Wales is now about 120,000; and that of the 120,000 cases of preventable suffering which thus, in every year, attain their final place in the death register, each unit represents a larger or smaller group of other cases in which preventable disease not ending in death, though often of far-reaching ill effects on life, has been suffered. And while these vast quantities of needless animal suffering, if regarded merely as such, would be a matter for indignant human protest, it further has to be remembered, as of legislative concern, that the physical strength of a people is an essential and main factor of national prosperity; that disease, so far as it affects the workers of the population, is in direct antagonism to industry; and that disease which affects the growing and reproductive parts of a population, must also in part be regarded as tending to deterioration of race." " Then there is the fact that this continuing tax on human life and welfare falls with immense over-proportion upon the most helpless classes of the community,—upon the poor, the ignorant, the subordinate, the immature : upon all classes which, in great part, through want of knowledge, and in great part because of their dependent position, cannot effectually remonstrate for themselves against the miseries thus brought upon them, and have in this circumstance the strongest of all claims on a legislature which can justly measure and can abate their sufferings."

# EXPLANATION OF THE PLATES.

FIG. 1.—Lockhead's ventilator. A pane of perforate glass, enclosed in a metal frame, with an extra fram hinged so as to exclude air, and provided with a regu lator to admit air as desired.

FIG. 2.—Expanding ventilator of wire gauze (attache to the upper sash of a window, in section) fitted wit joints and made to double up.

FIG. 3.—Grate with valves, *a a*, to admit cold air i proximity to the fire; *b*, a channel below the floor t provide air from an external source. Much of this a becomes warmed, and circulates in the room.

FIG. 3 *a*.—Horizontal section across the upper part a grate, to admit air through open sprandrils, *a a*, th air passing through an external source to the back of th grate, and becoming there heated before entering th room.

FIG. 4 *a*.—Perforated zinc ventilator adapted to forn part of a cornice; *f*, perforated zinc.

FIG. 4 is the same in section as applied to a room *a*, air brick in external wall; *b*, under part of corni facing the room; *c*, portion of cornice over the apertu by which air is admitted from without; *d*, cord to regu late admission of air through; *e*, door or valve.

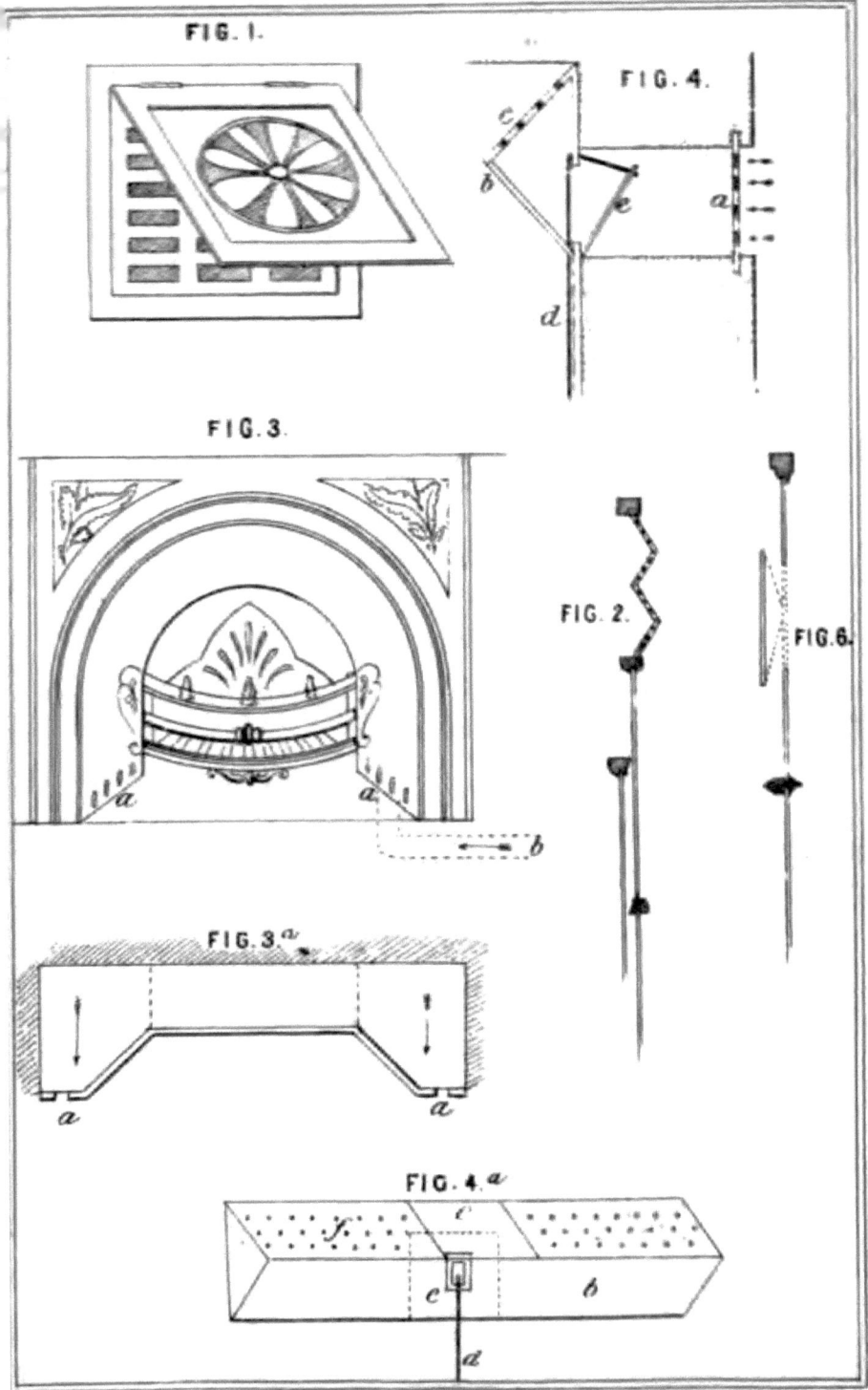

FIG. 1.

FIG. 4.

FIG. 3.

FIG. 2.

FIG. 6.

FIG. 3.ᵃ

FIG. 4.ᵃ

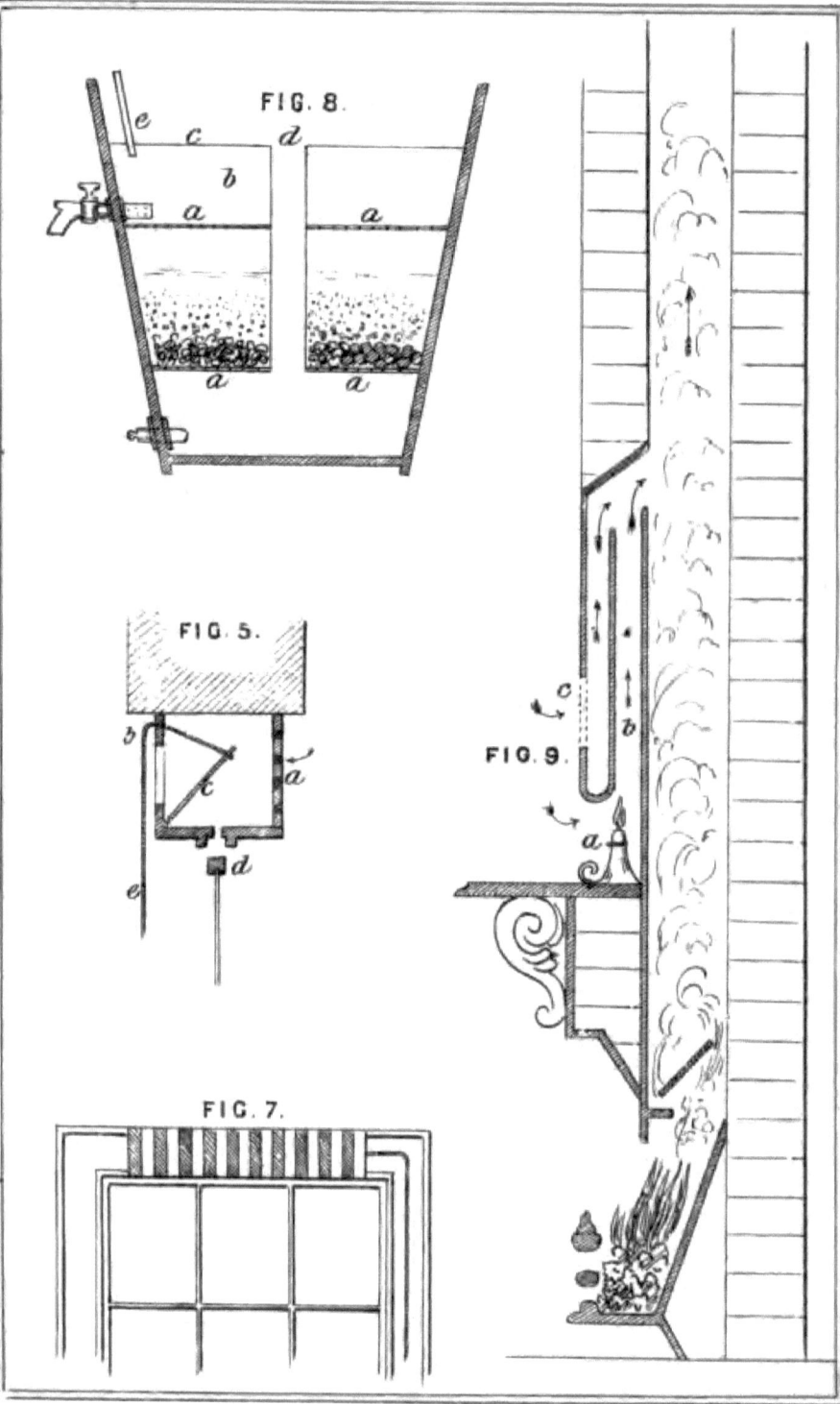

FIG. 8.

FIG. 5.

FIG. 9.

FIG. 7.

Fig. 5.—Vertical section, showing an arrangement for supplying air at the top part of a window independently of the sash ; *a*, perforated external apertures ; *b*, gauze facing the room ; *c*, plate to regulate admission of air ; *d*, window sash slightly lowered ; *e*, cord to move *c*.

Fig. 6.—Boyle's window ventilator consists of a disc of glass attached to an opening, covered with wire gauze, in the window frame, by jointed rods, by which the distance of the disc from the gauze can be regulated.

Fig. 7.—Gammon's ventilator fixed to a window sash. This is a narrow box, having a perforated face of brass, and a similar back of zinc. The face is divided into compartments, alternately perforated and plain. A similar plate is made to move over the perforated parts by means of a cord and pulley, to admit or exclude air.

Fig. 8.—Section of a filter ; *a a*, plates of perforated metal, between which is the filtering material; *b*, reservoir for the filtered water ; *c*, covering ; *d*, tube for the conveyance of water for filtration ; *e*, air tube.

Fig. 9.—Section of the ventilating lamp or chimney of the Marquis de Chambaunes ; *a*, lamp ; *b*, channel to chimney ; *c*, aperture protected by wire gauze through which the air of the room passes to the chimney.

JOHNSON AND TESSEYMAN, PRINTERS, YORK.